I0783681

FAST FRIENDS

Dale Lazarov & Michael Broderick

StickyGraphicNovels.com

Printed and distributed by
ComicMix, LLC.,
71 Hauxhurst Ave. Suite B
Weehawken, NJ 07086.
http://www.comicmix.com

Printed in USA.

Hardcover ISBN: 978-1-939888-57-0

script / edits / art direction : Dale Lazarov
layouts / linework / colors : Michael Broderick

dia
HOTEL

SORDID
ROMANCE

LIQUOR

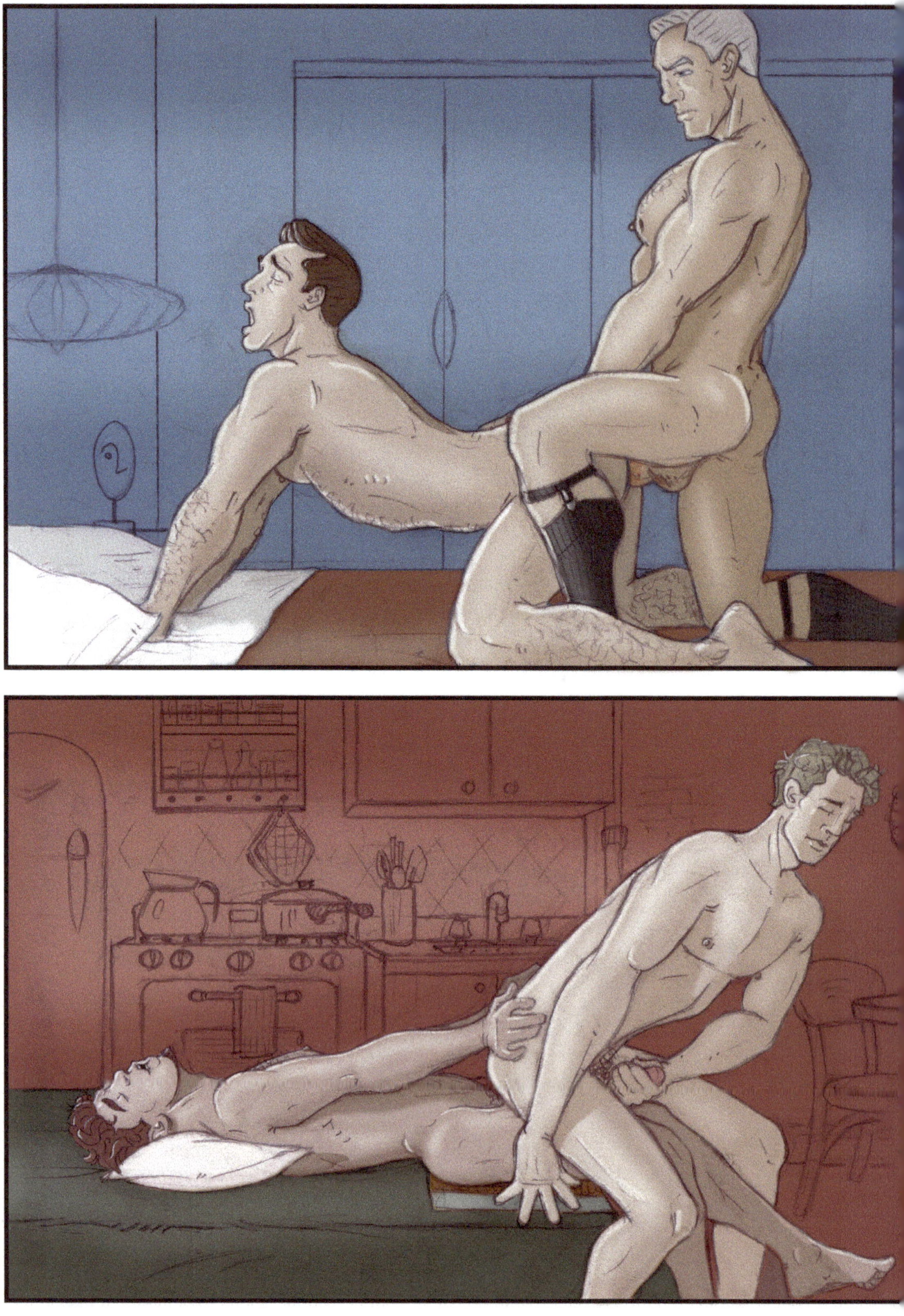

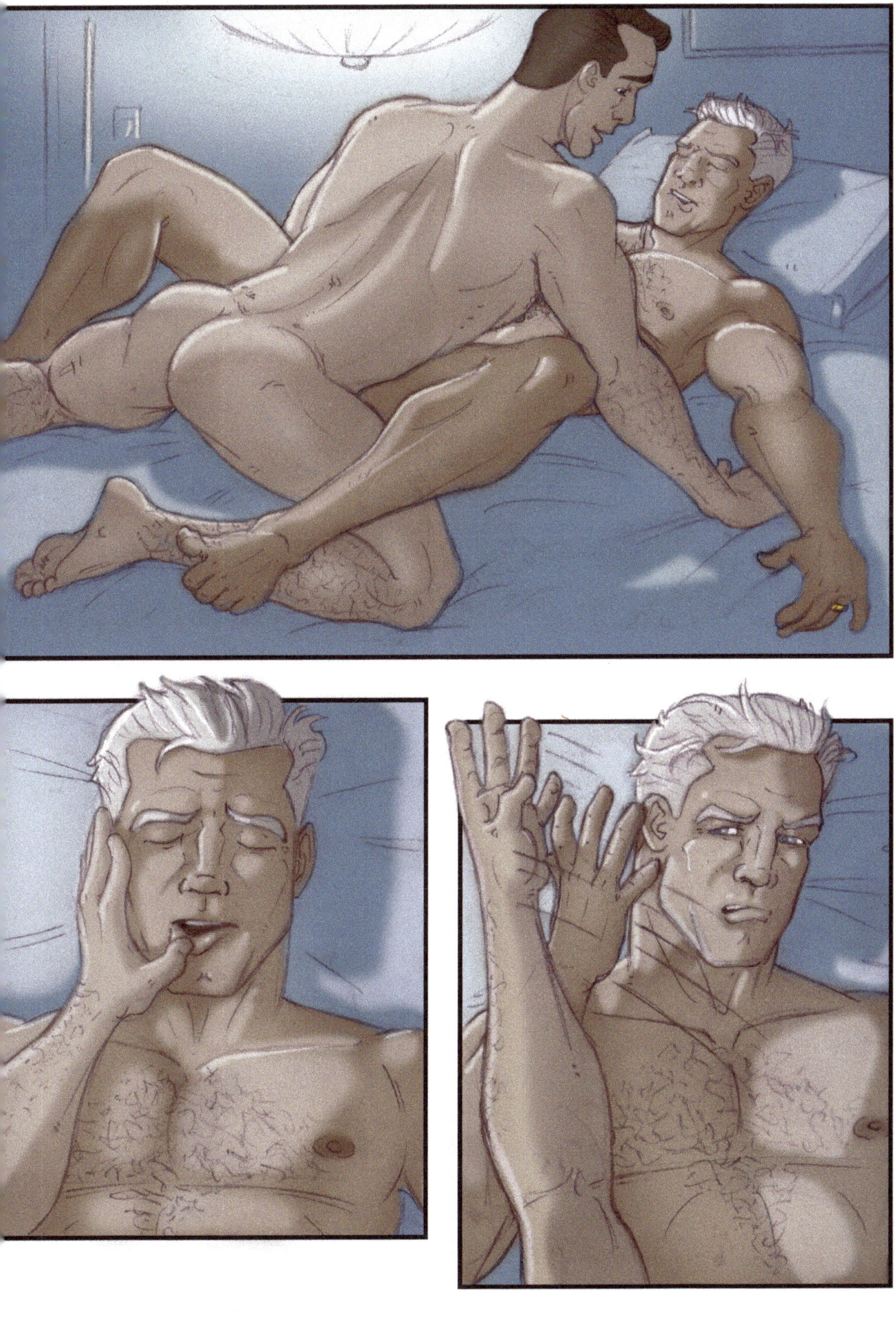

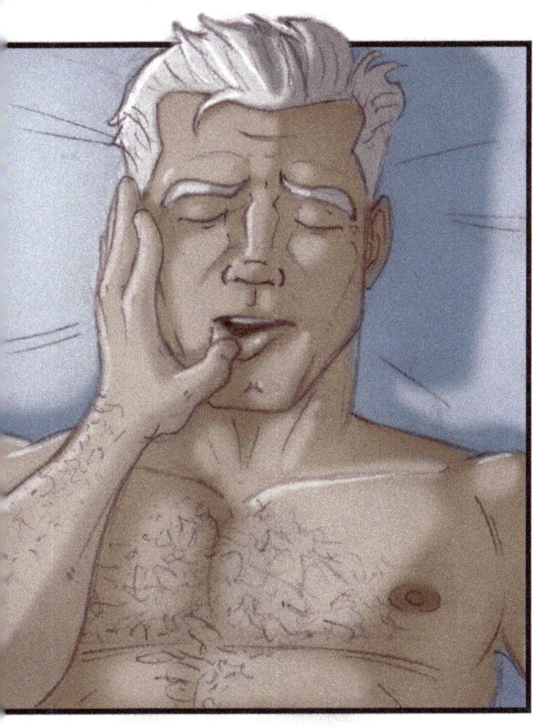
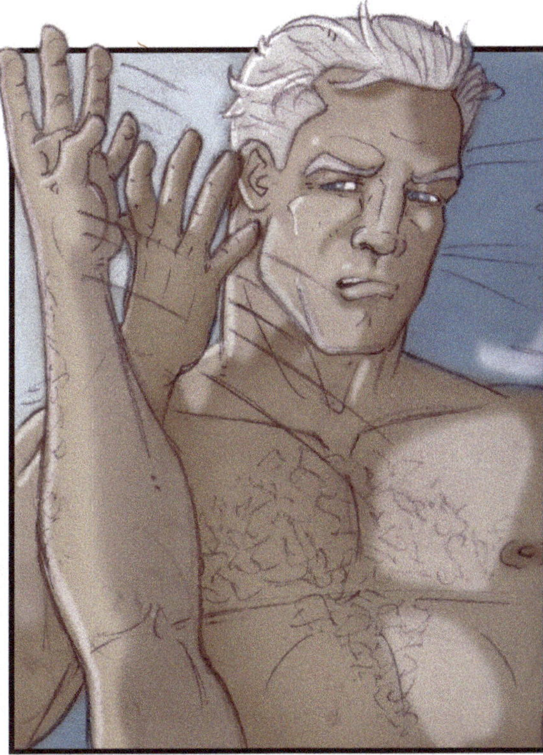

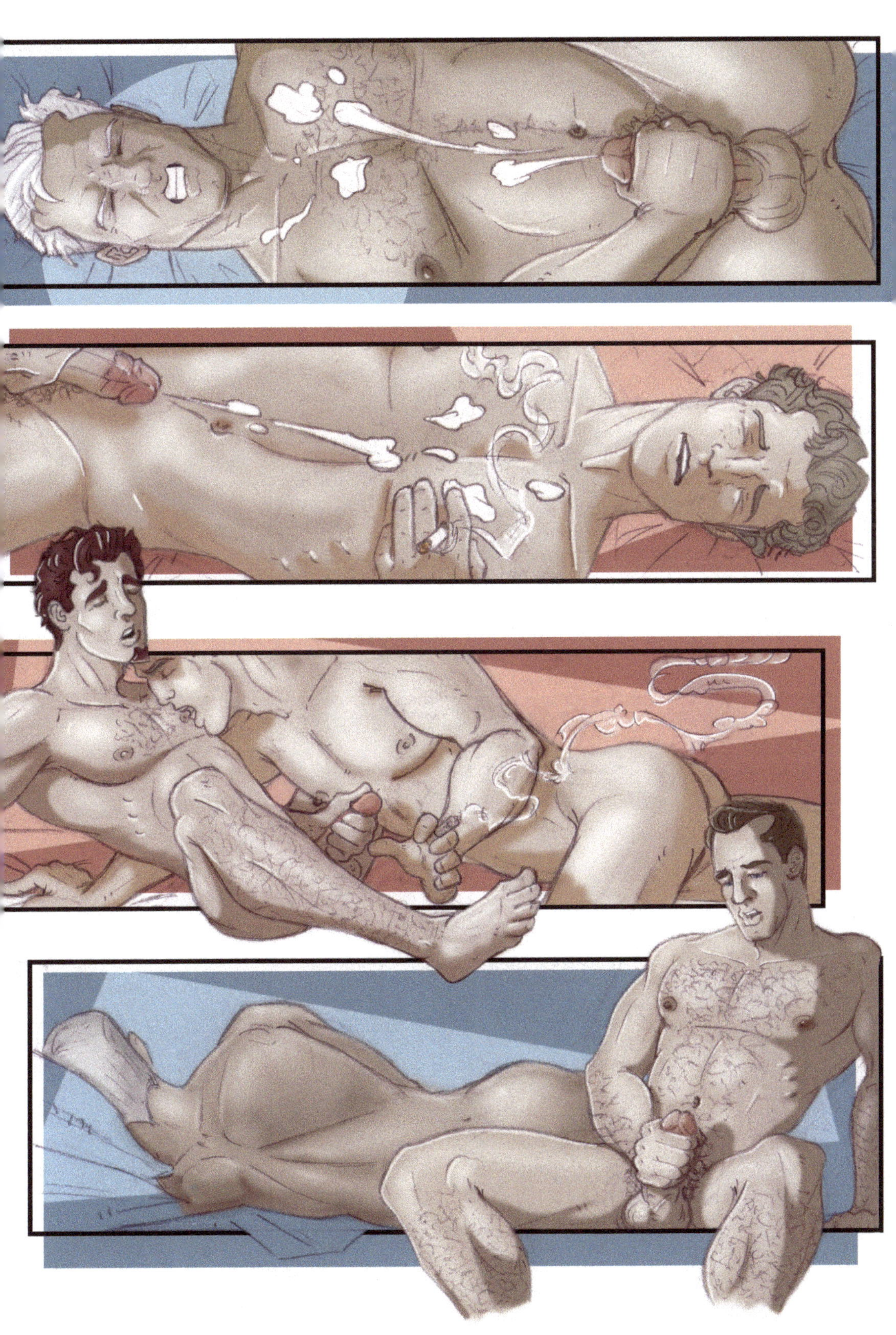

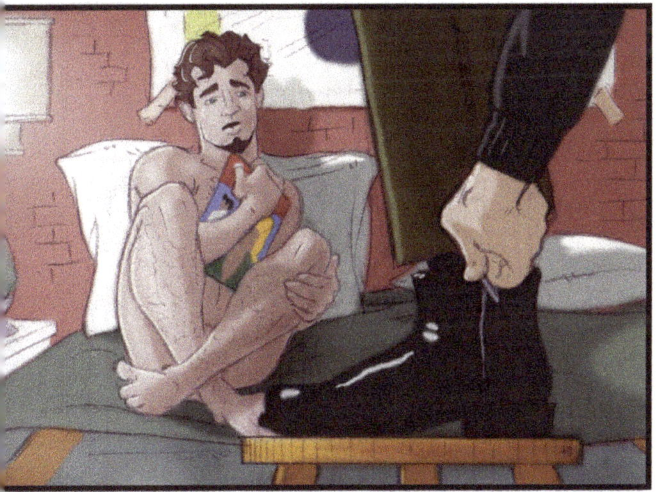

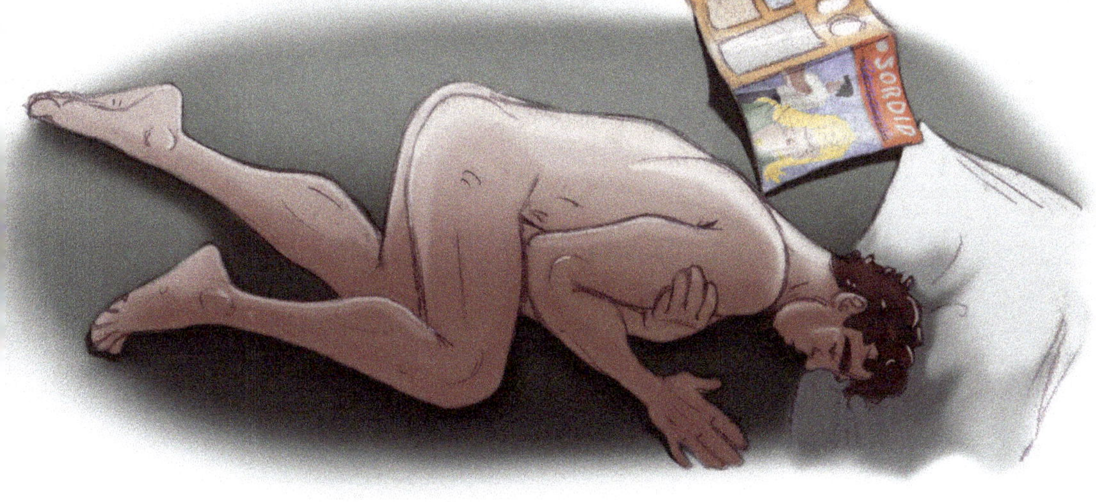
SORDID

49SRUK

COFFEE
Nick's NEWS & MAGAZINE
Nick's
74

ATTACK OF THE 50 FT. WOMAN
MAGAZINES
COMICS
10¢

COMICS 10¢
10¢

COLD BLOODED

NORTH ST
Dale's
LUNCHEONETTE
CANDY · SODA

DALE

SPECIALS

MENU

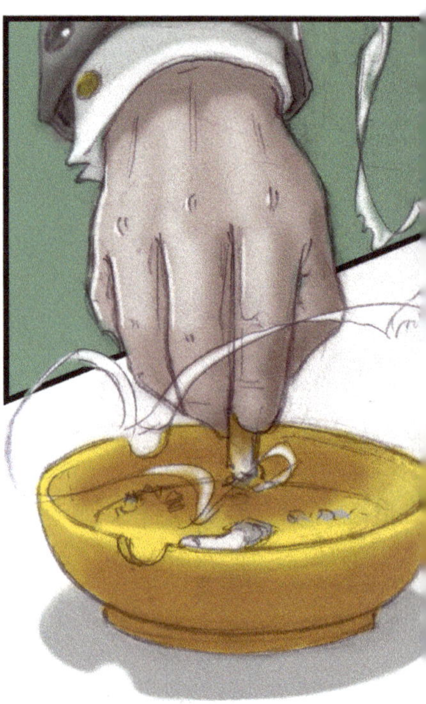
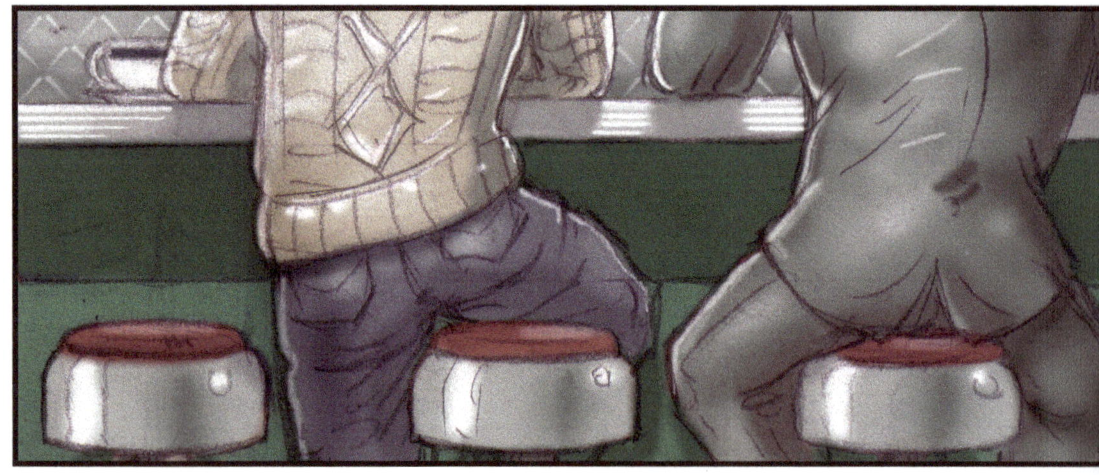

SPECIALS

ROCKWELL
PUB
FATALE

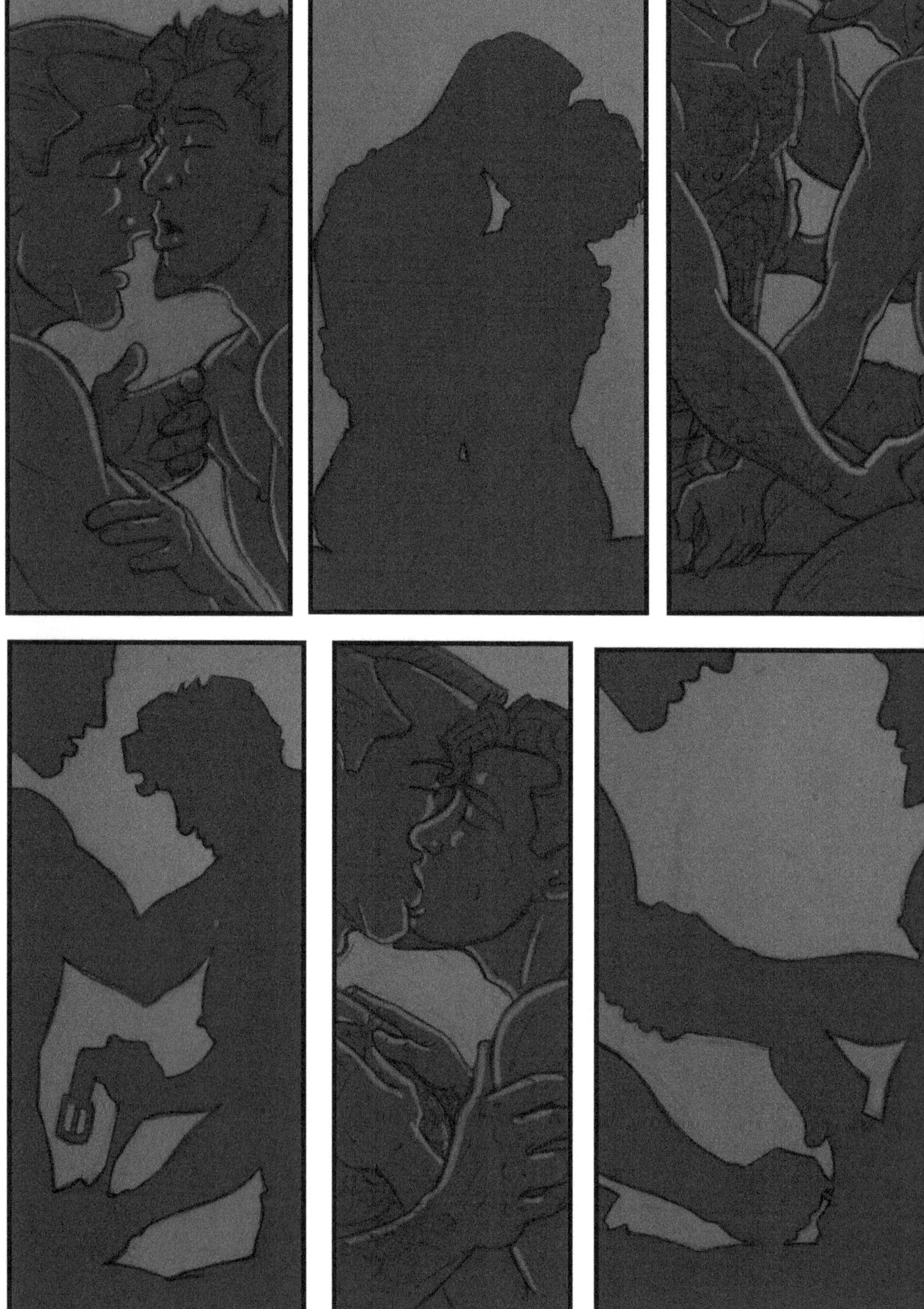

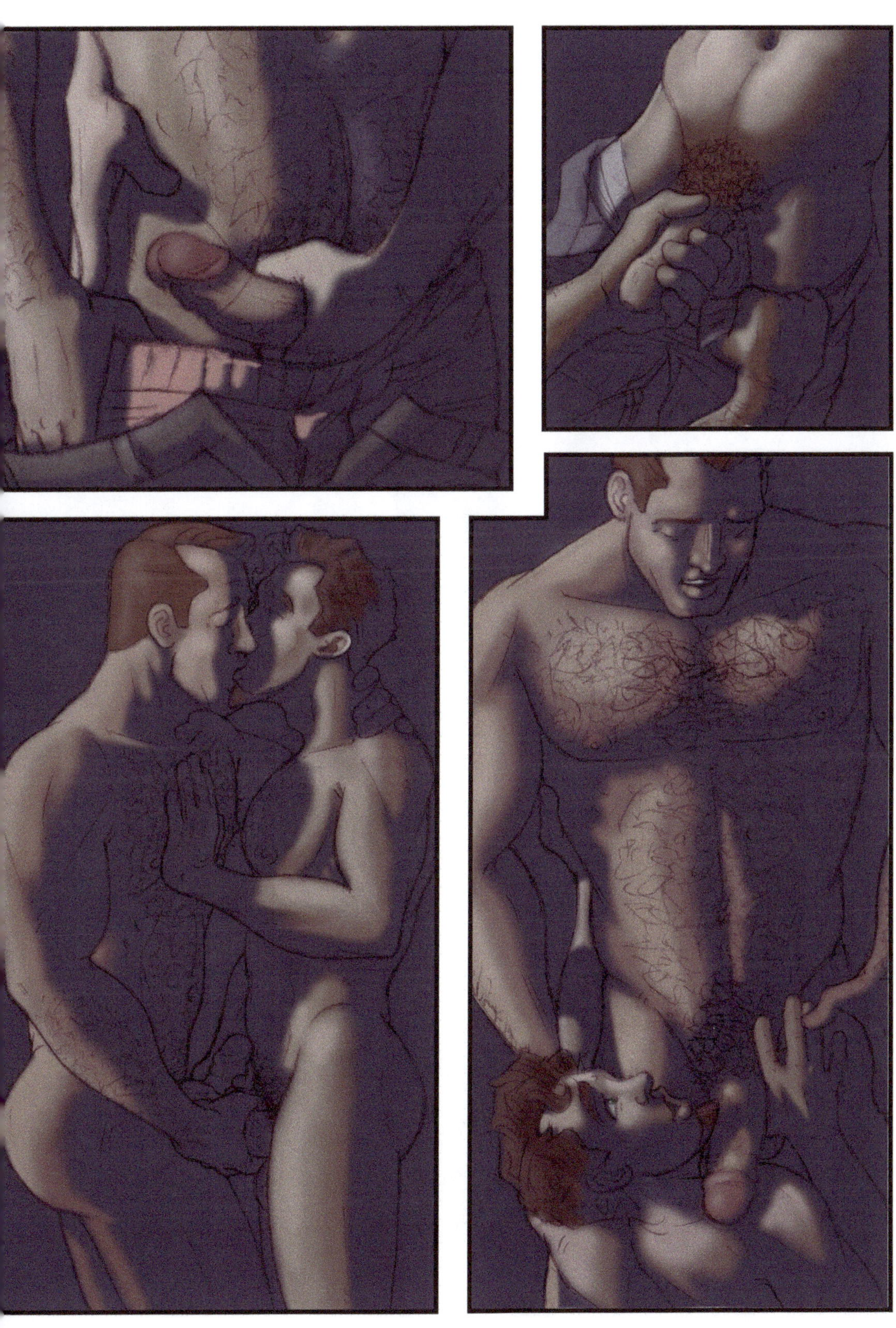

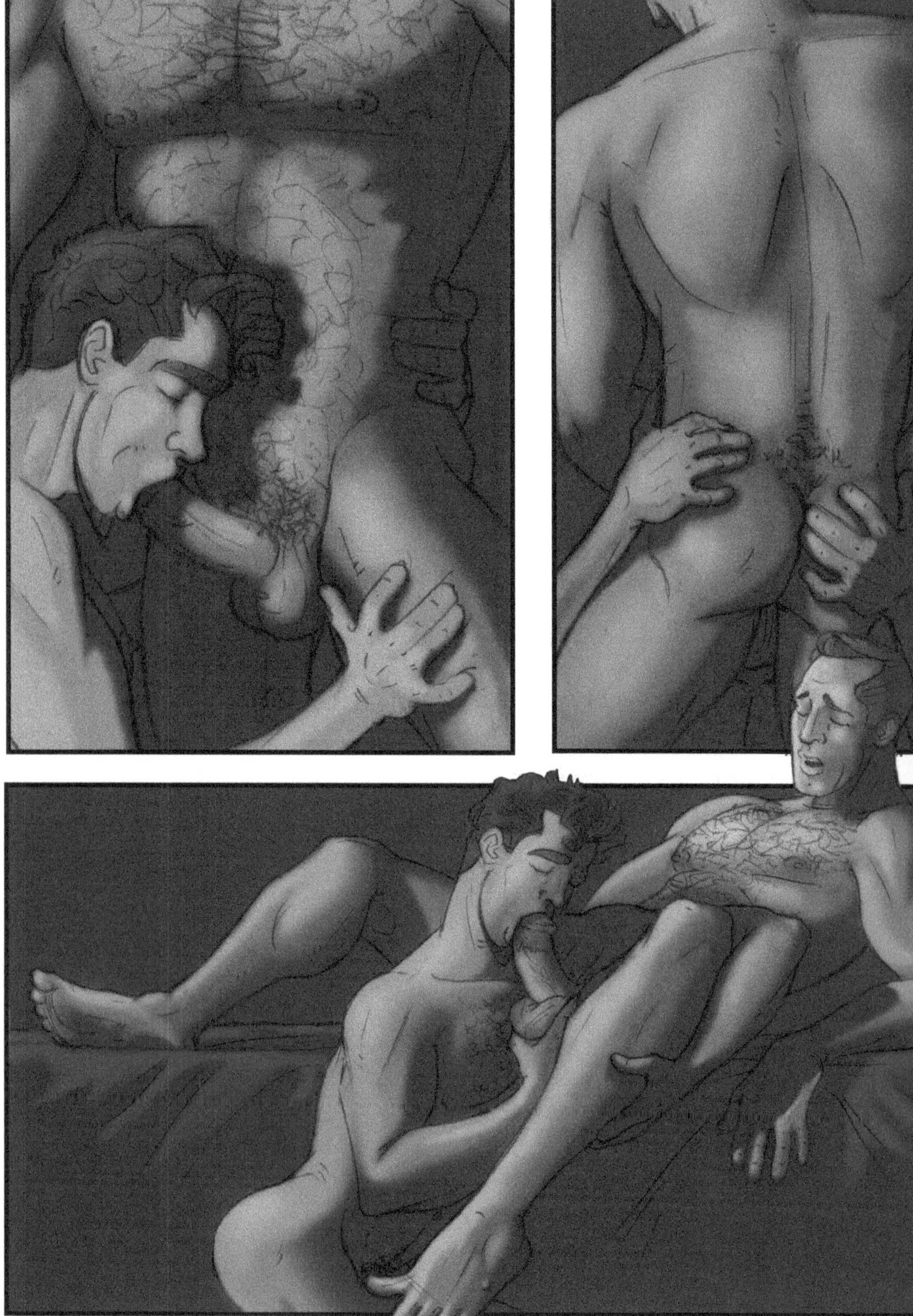

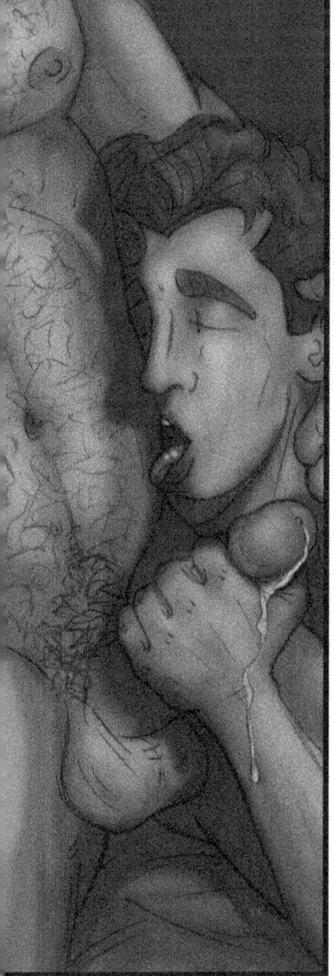

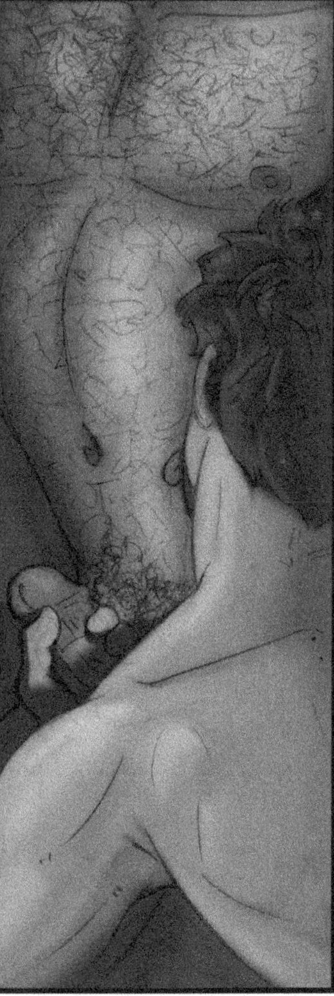

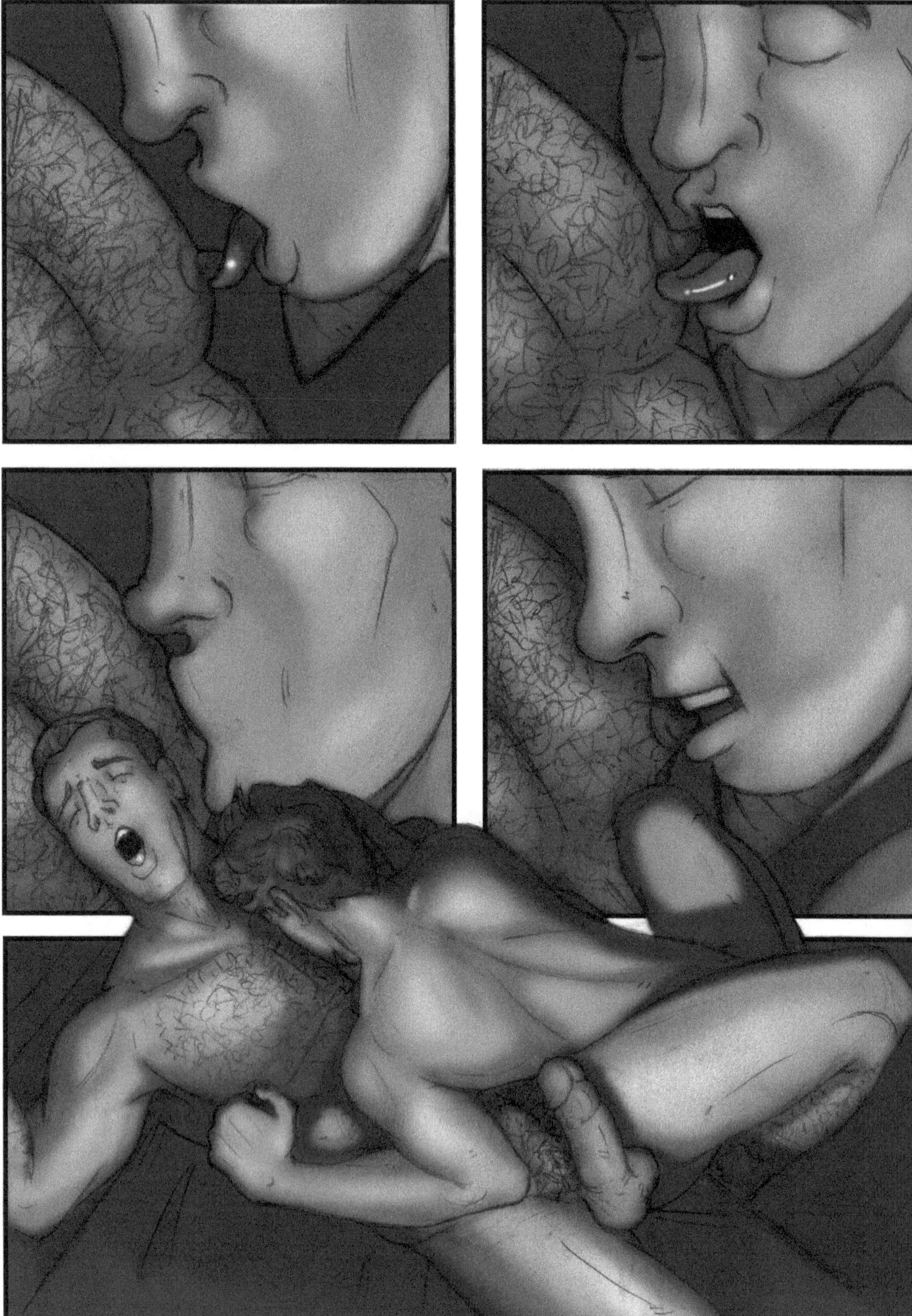

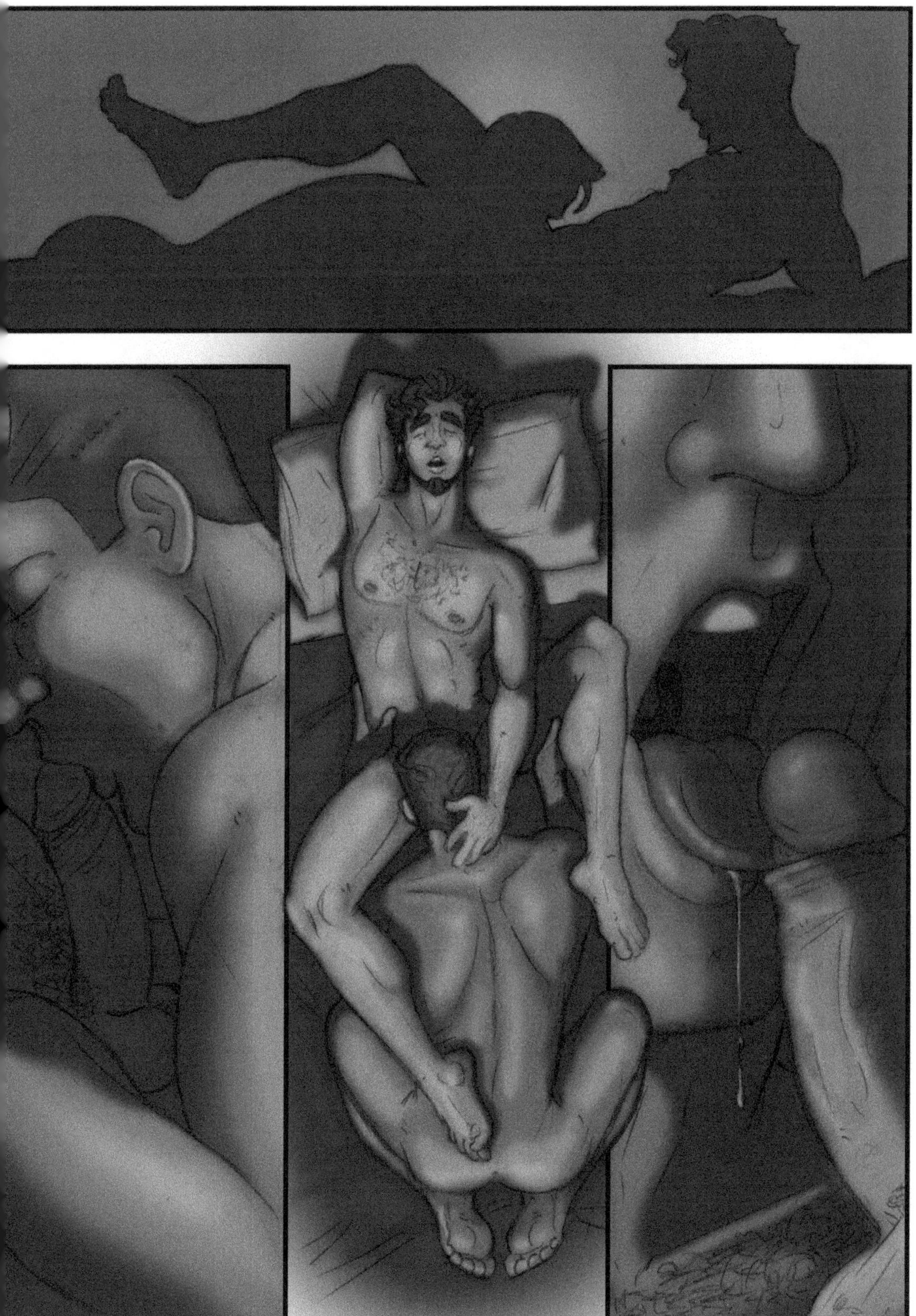

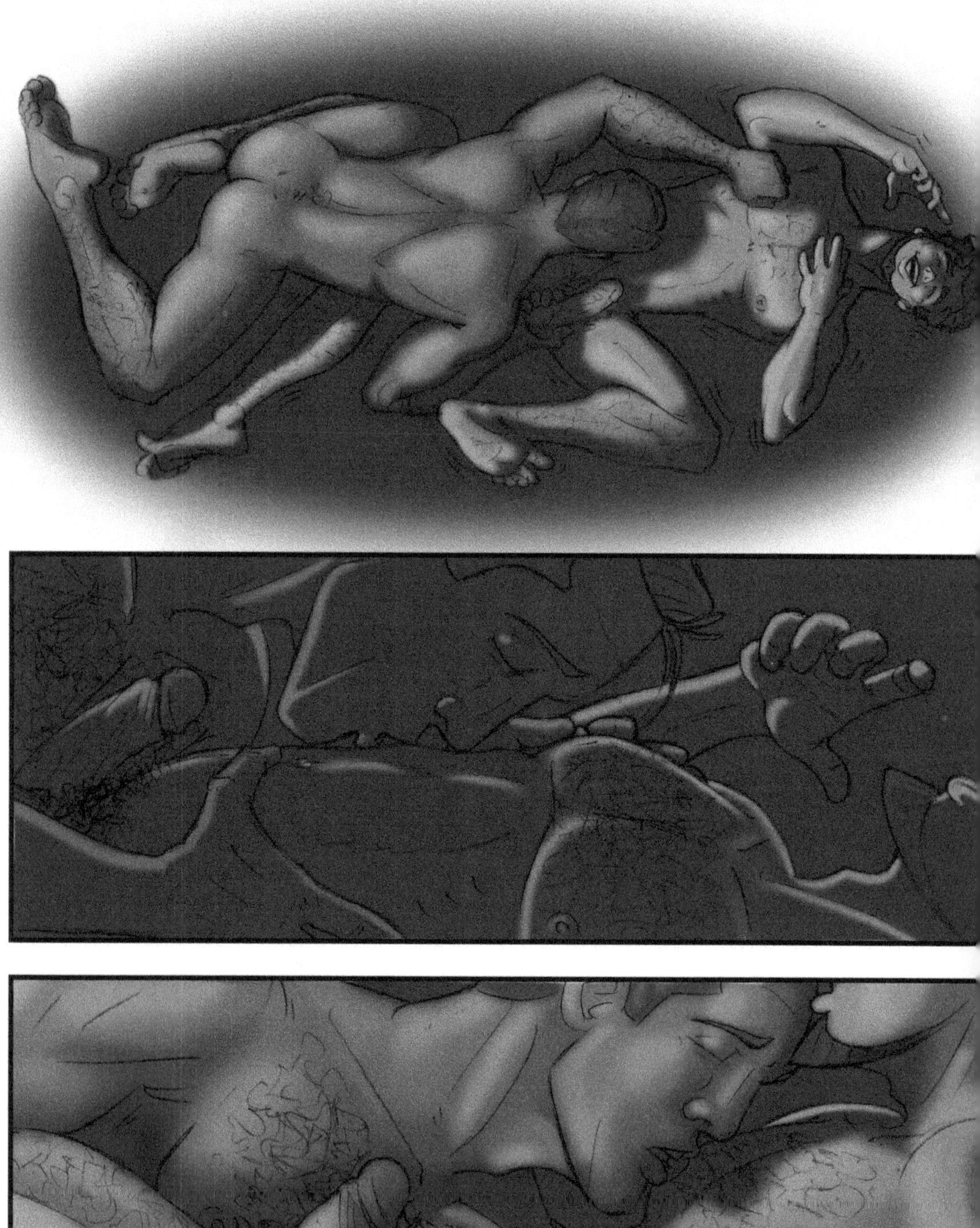

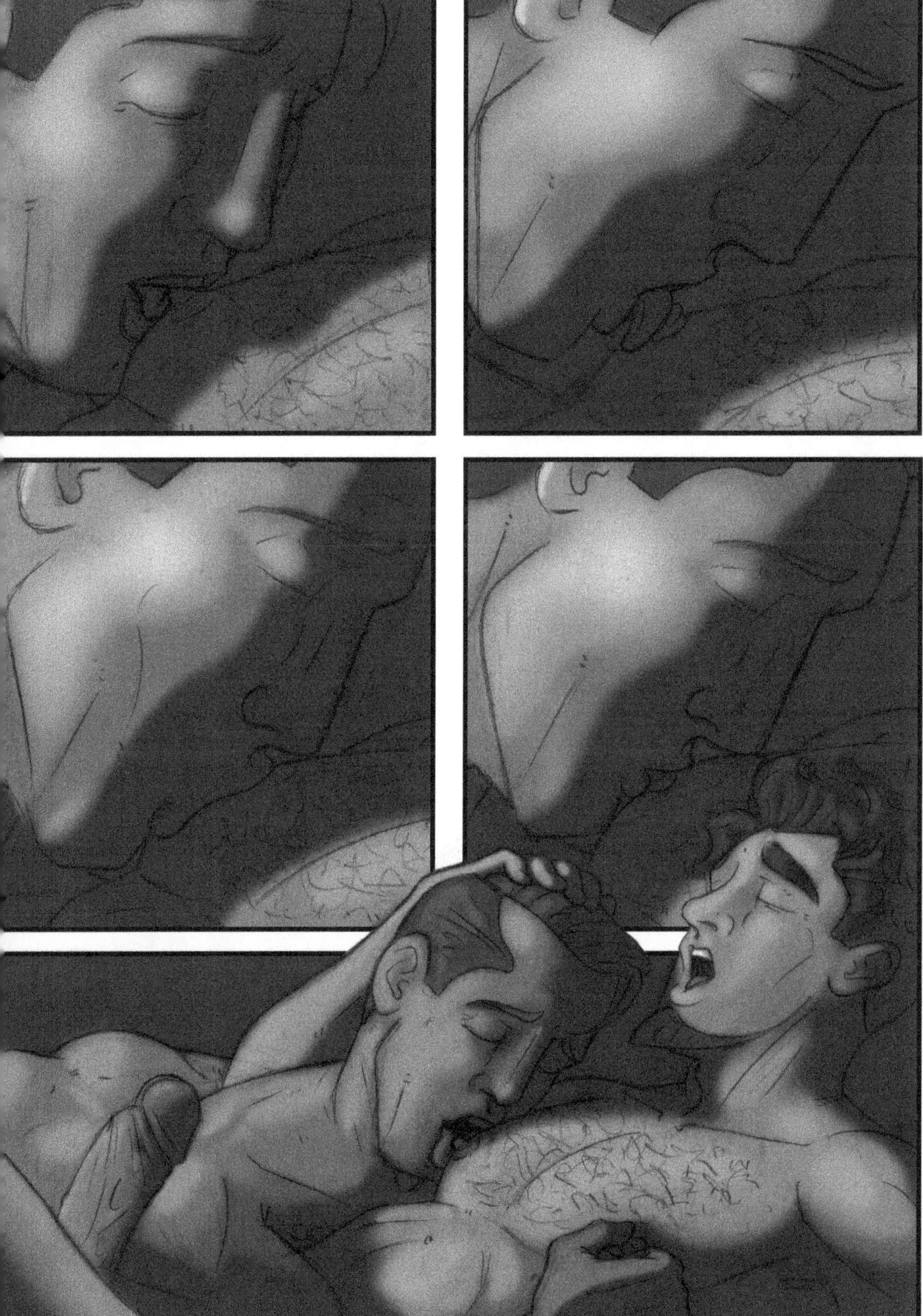

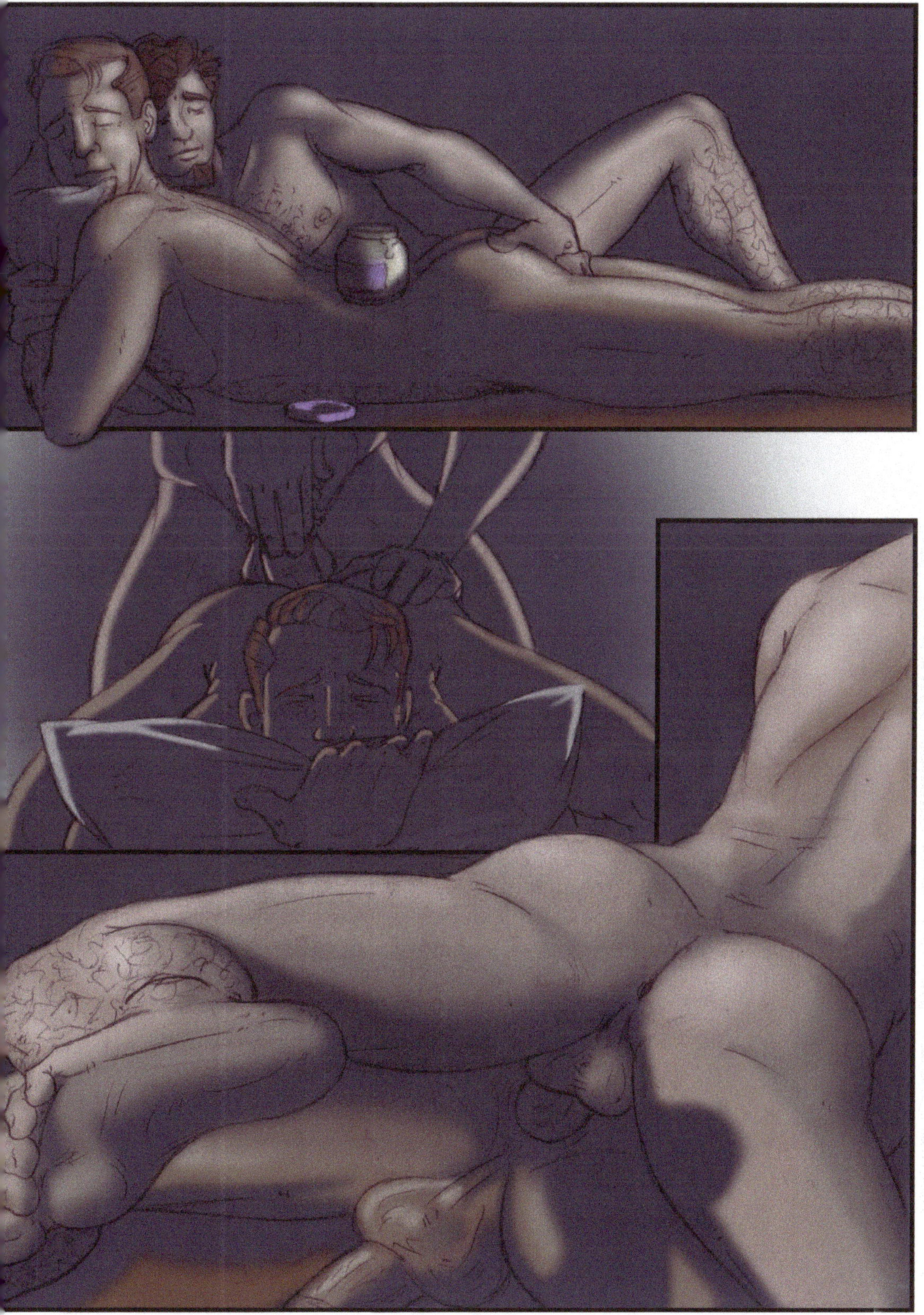

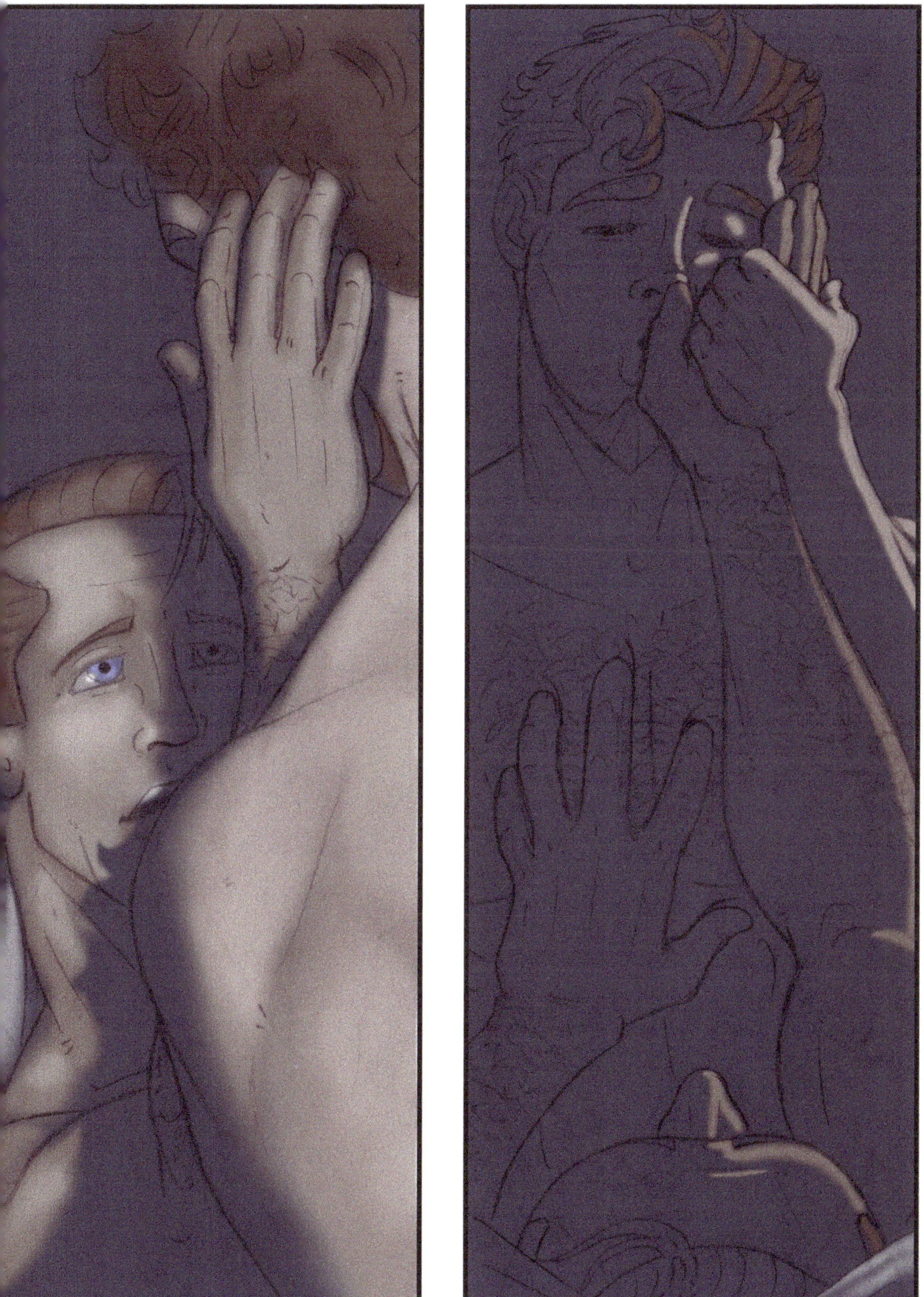

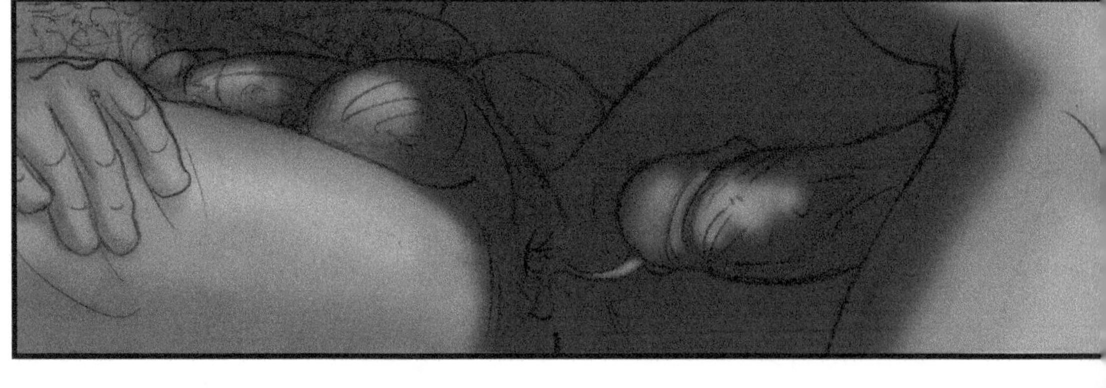

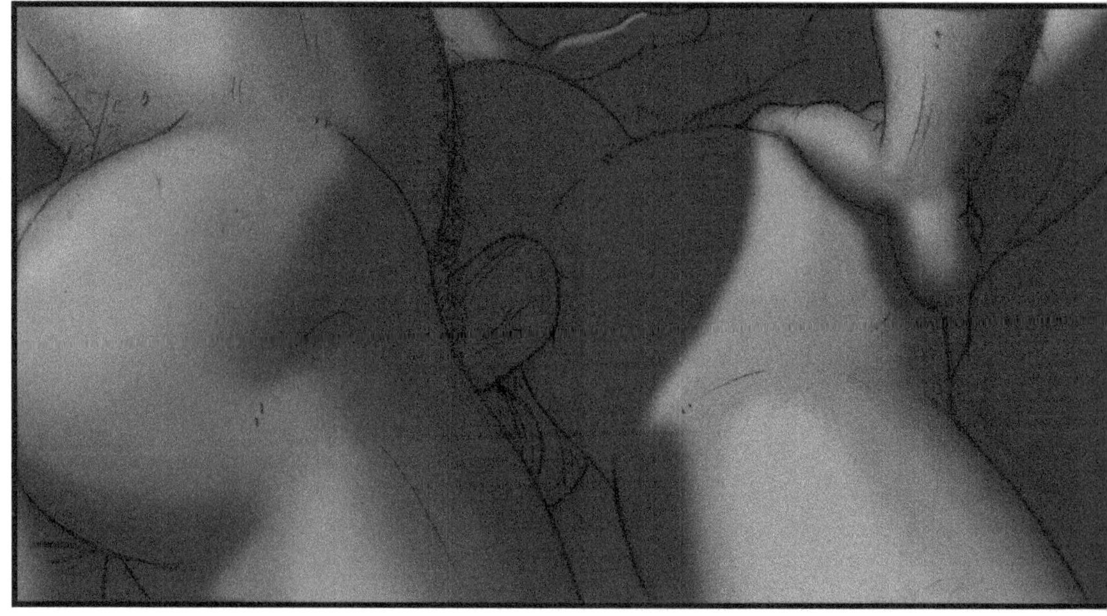

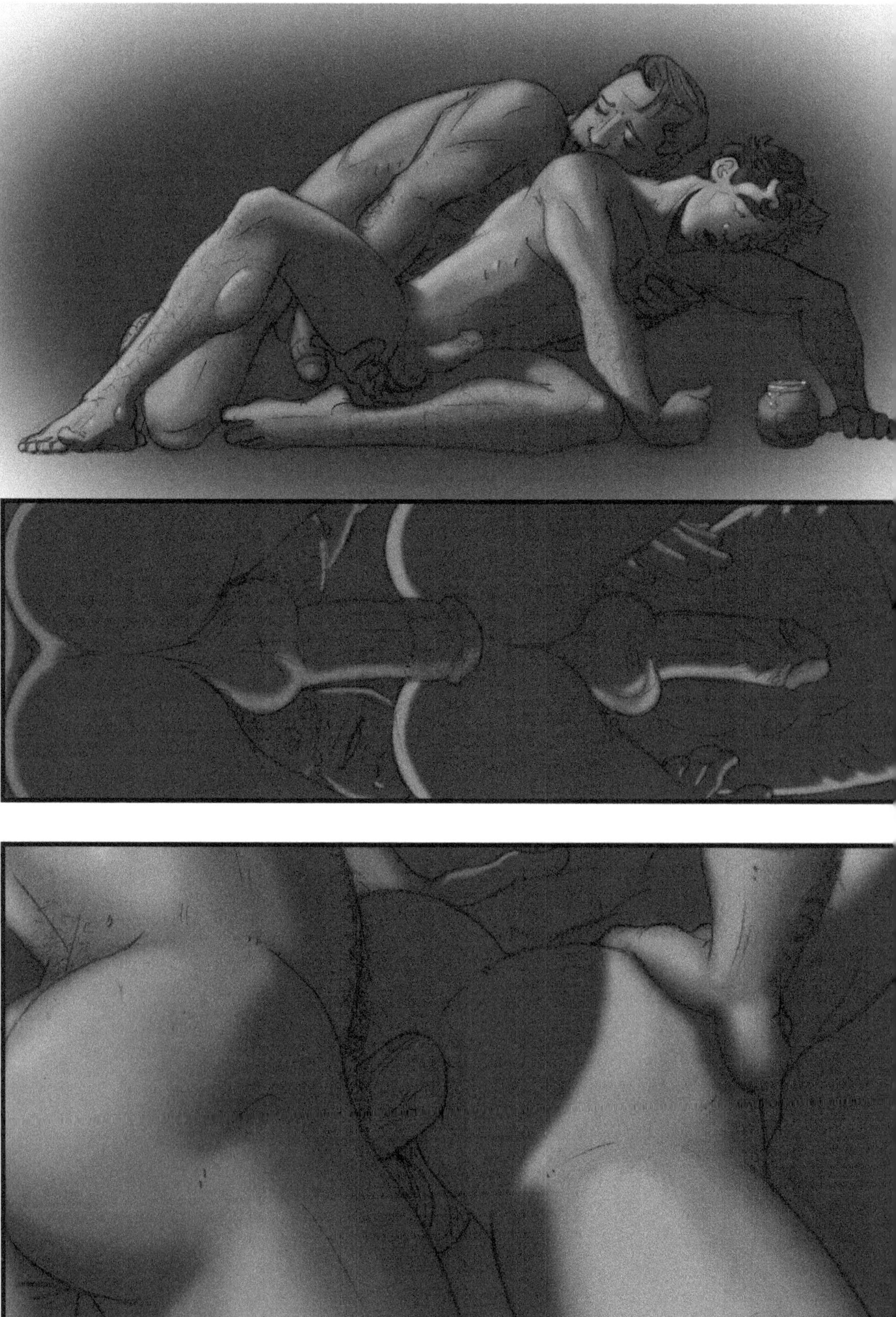

3F
TAWDRY LIVES

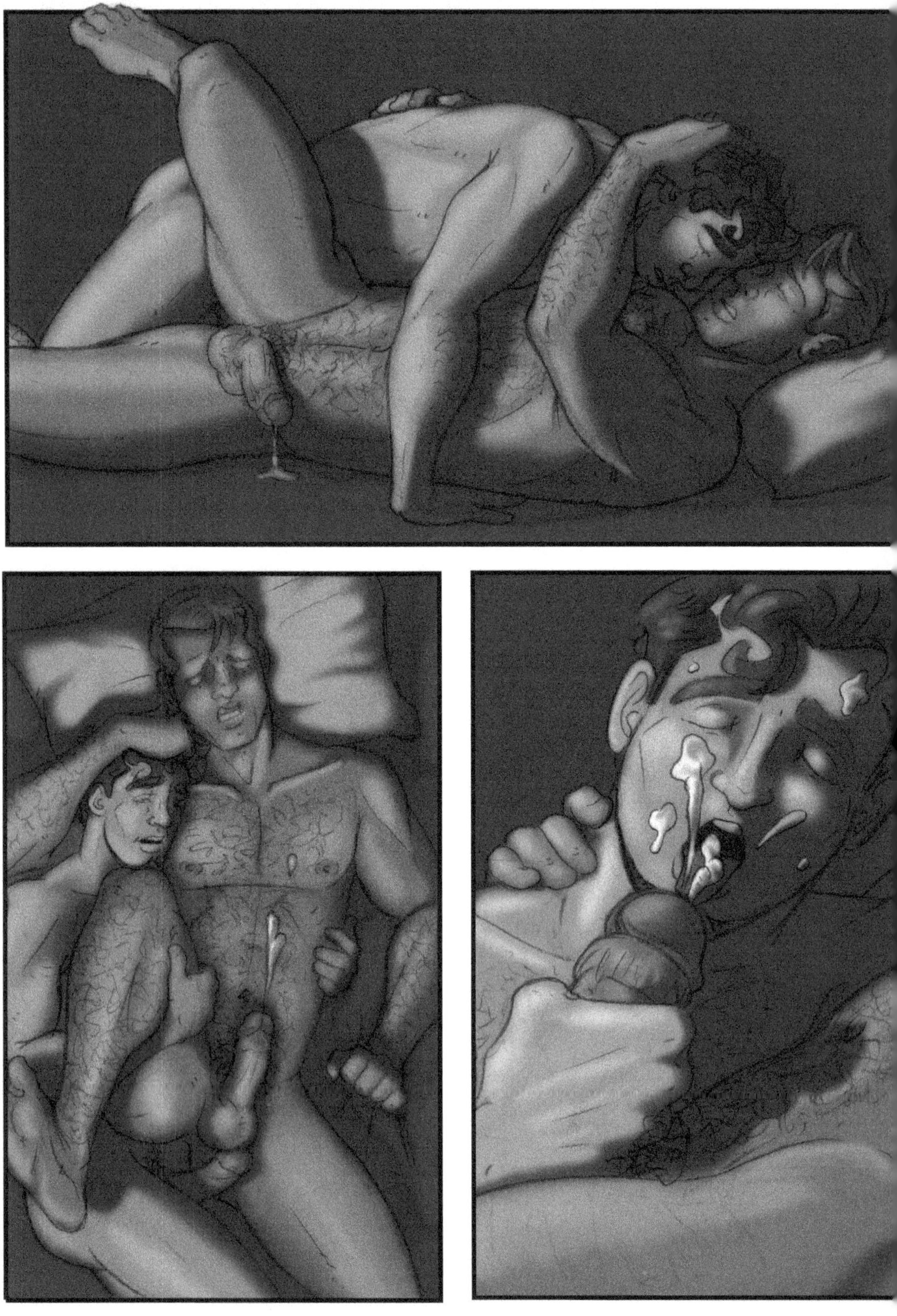

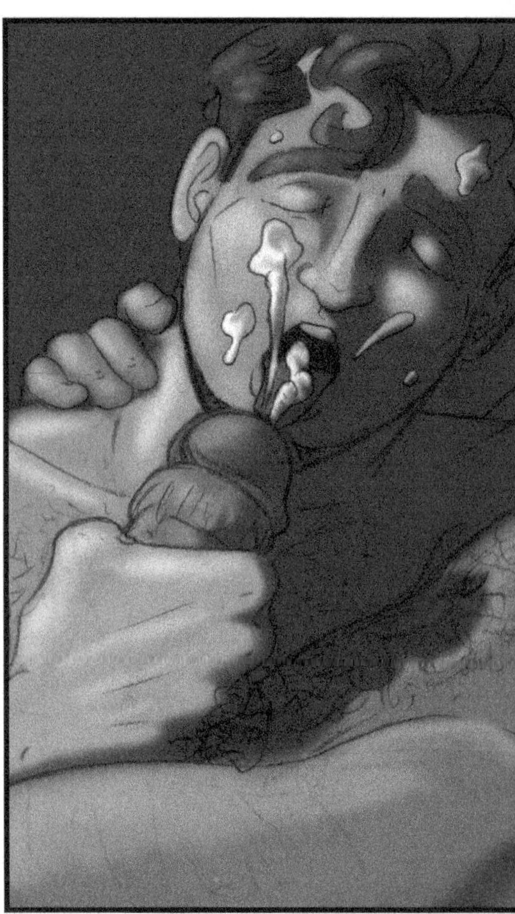

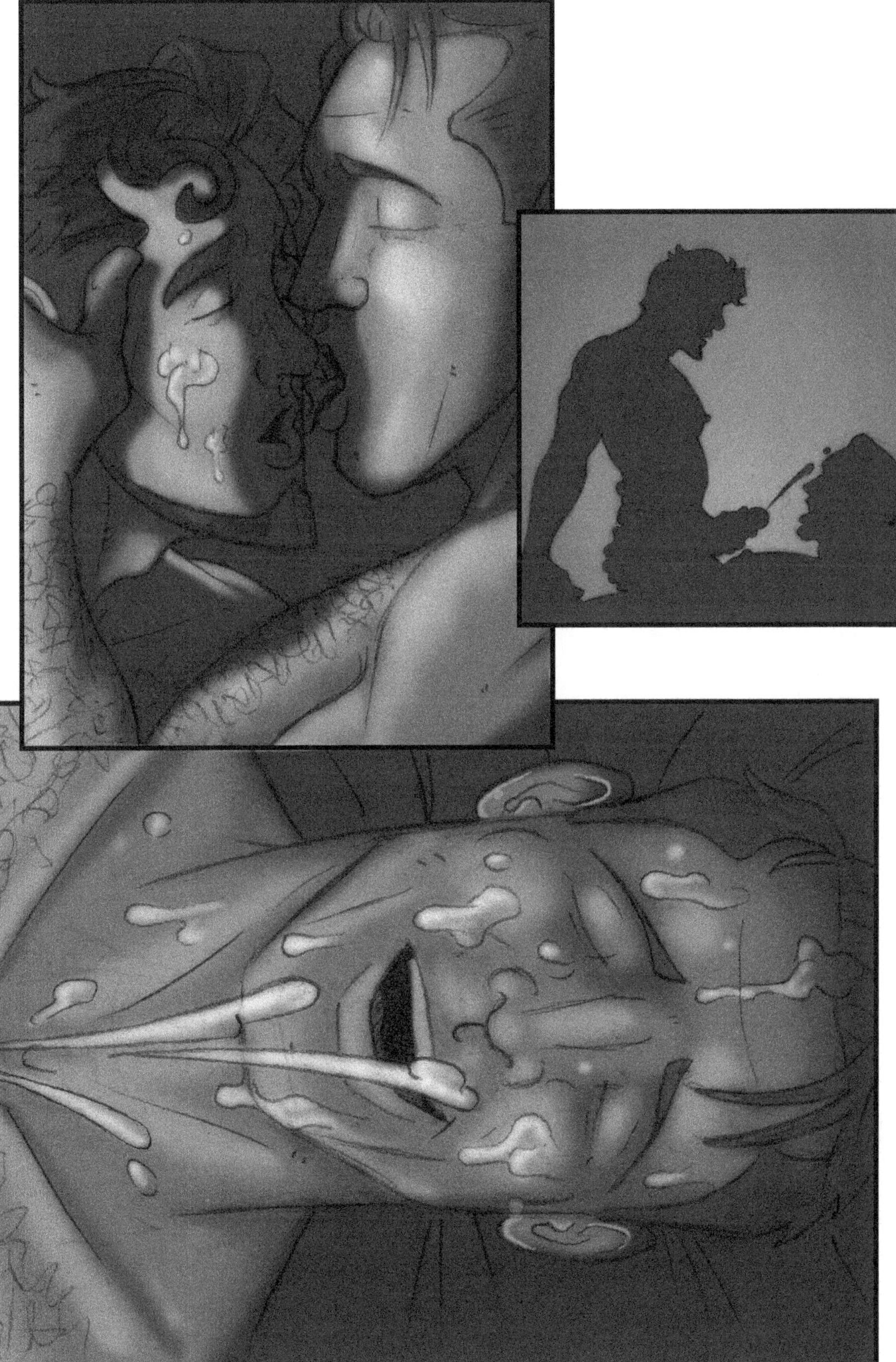

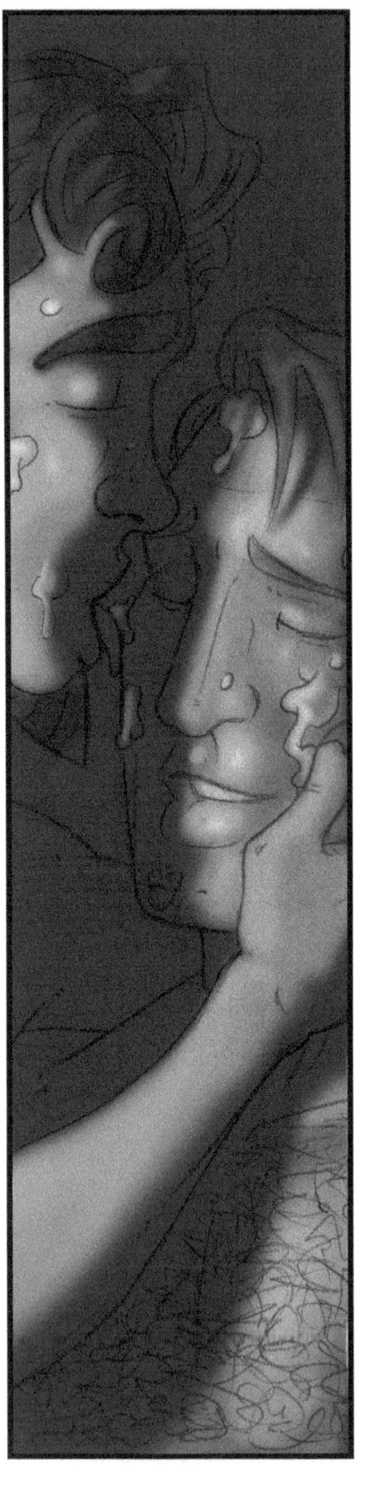
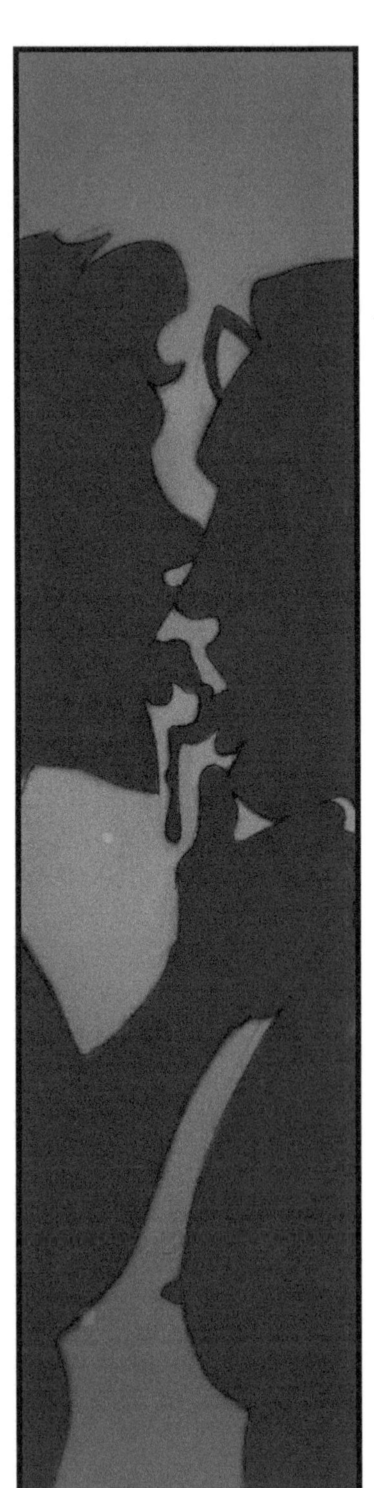
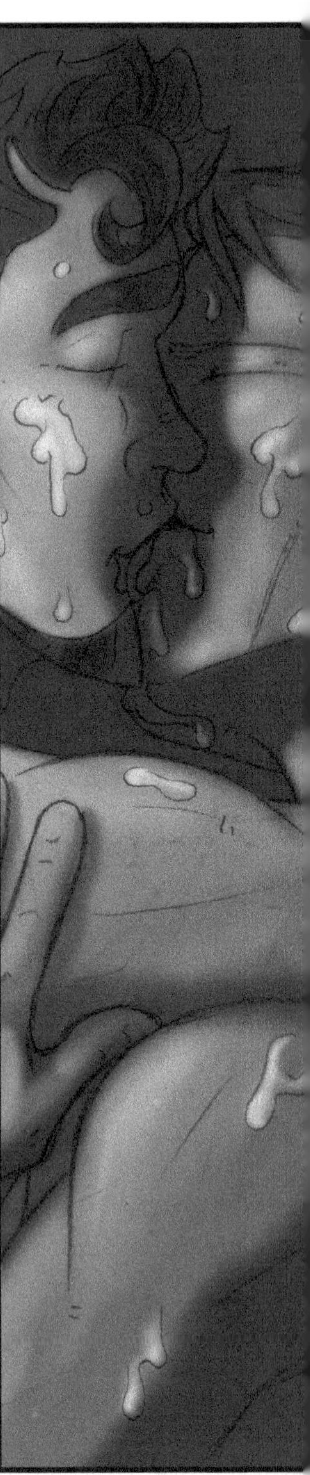

ARMEN
RANDA
IN RIO
NICOLOR

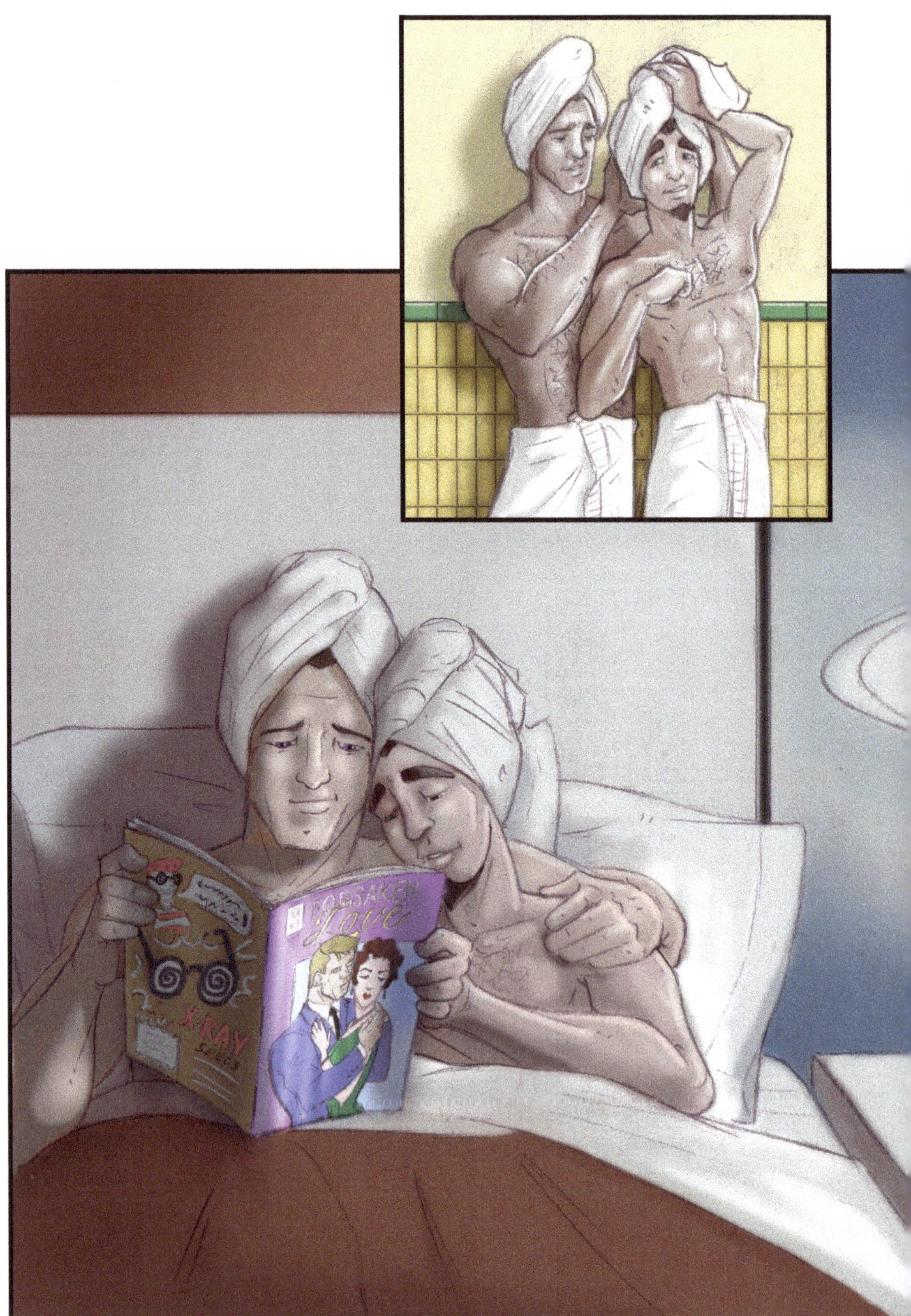
FORSAKEN
love
X-RAY
SPECS

END

About The Authors:

Dale Lazarov is the writer, art director and licensor of Sticky Graphic Novels
-- wordless, gay character-based, sex-positive graphic novels for an international
audience. Since 2006, he has collaborated on 12 hardcover Sticky Graphic Novels
and 39 digital editions with distinctive and evocative gay comics artists from around
the globe. He lives in Chicago.

Michael Broderick escaped a dreary existence in upstate New York in his late teens,
moved to New York City and got a BA in Graphic Art and Drawing at School of
Visual Art. Inspired by hunks of yesteryear like Mike Henry, Guy Madison and
Gene Kelly, Michael's work seeks to conjure images conspicuously absent for
those of us who grew up gay in America. In the last 20 years, Michael's work as
appeared in a number of erotic art anthologies and has published two books, *Just
Us Guys* and *G Is For Groundskeeper*, published by Bruno Gmunder. Michael has
had solo gallery shows in Philadelphia and Amsterdam, and, most recently, had
work in *Stroke: From Under The Mattress To The Museum Walls*, an exhibition
at the Leslie Lohman Museum of Gay and Lesbian Art in New York City. Visit his
website at hottlead.com.